Great Illustrated Classics

BLACK BEAUTY

Anna Sewell

adapted by
Deidre Laiken

BARONET BOOKS

BARONET BOOKS, New York, New York

GREAT ILLUSTRATED CLASSICS

edited by
Malvina G. Vogel

Printed in the United States of America

CONTENTS

CHAPTER PAGE

1. My First Home 9
2. My Breaking In 17
3. Birtwick Park 29
4. Freedom 35
5. Ginger 39
6. Ginger's Story Continued 47
7. Merrylegs 53
8. A Talk in the Orchard 59
9. A Stormy Day 69
10. James Howard 83
11. The Fire 89
12. James Leaves Birtwick Park 101
13. Going for the Doctor 107
14. Leaving Home 117

15. Our New Home 123
16. Rebellion 133
17. Reuben Smith 139
18. How It Ended 147
19. Ruined and Going Downhill 153
20. A Thief 163
21. A Horse Fair 169
22. A City Cab Horse 175
23. Jerry Barker 181
24. Poor Ginger 187
25. Jerry's New Year 195
26. Jakes and the Old Woman 205
27. Hard Times 211
28. Farmer Thoroughgood and His Grandson ... 223
29. My Last Home 229

About the Author

Anna Sewell was born in Yarmouth, England in 1820. It took her nearly seven years to write *Black Beauty*, her only book.

The author learned to know and love horses when she was a young girl. Driving her father to and from the train station in a pony cart, she was able to observe both people and their horses. After a serious fall in which she was badly hurt, she could no longer ride.

Despite her pain, Anna Sewell was determined to complete her novel. She dictated much of the book to her mother, who wrote it all down when Anna was too weak to hold a pencil.

Black Beauty was published in 1877. Anna Sewell died a year later. The book was popular from the start. It called people's attention to their often cruel and thoughtless treatment of animals and did much to improve conditions for all animals.

Horses You Will Meet

Black Beauty

Duchess, *Black Beauty's mother*

Merrylegs, *the pony*

Ginger, *the spirited chestnut mare*

Sir Oliver

Captain

The People Black Beauty Meets

Black Beauty's First Master

Squire Gordon, *the owner of Birtwick Park*

John and James, *the stable grooms*

Joe Green, *the young groom*

Mr. York of Earlshall Park

The New Mistress

Reuben Smith

Mr. Barry, *Black Beauty's third owner*

Filcher and the Young Boy

Jerry Barker, *the city cab driver*

Polly, *his wife*

Dolly, *his daughter*

Jakes, *the driver for the corn dealer*

Nicholas Skinner, *the cruel owner of the cab fleet*

Mr. Thoroughgood, *the good farmer*

Willie, *his grandson*

Miss Ellen and Her Two Sisters

In the Shade of the Trees

Chapter 1
My First Home

When I look back, my first memories are of a large rolling meadow with a small pond. Green, shady trees leaned over the pond, and water lilies grew in the deep end.

As a colt, I was too young to eat grass so I lived on my mother's milk. In the daytime I ran at her side and at night I slept beside her. During the warm weather we used to stand by the pond in the shade of the trees. In the winter we went to a warm shed near an apple orchard.

There were six colts in the meadow besides

me. They were all older than I was. Some were almost as large as grown-up horses. I used to have great fun running with them. Sometimes we would bite and kick as well as run.

One day when there was a lot of kicking my mother whinnied to me to come to her, and she said:

"I hope you will grow up gentle and good and never learn bad ways. Do your work well, lift up your feet when you trot, and never bite or kick, even when you are just playing."

I never forgot my mother's advice. I knew she was a wise horse, and our master loved her very much. Her name was Duchess, but he often called her Pet.

Our master was a good man. He gave us good food, a good home, and kind words. He talked to us as if we were his children. We all loved him very much. When my mother

Colts in the Meadow

saw him at the gate she would neigh with joy and run up to him. He would pat and stroke her and say, "Well, old Pet, how is your little Blackie?" I was a dull black so he called me "Blackie." Then he would give me a piece of bread and my mother a carrot. All the horses would come to him, but I think we were his favorites. My mother always took him to the town on market day in a small carriage.

There was a young boy named Dick who sometimes came into our field to pluck blackberries from the tree. After he had eaten all he wanted he would throw sticks and stones at the colts. He thought this was fun. But sometimes a stone would hit us, and it hurt a great deal.

One day when he was doing this, he did not know that my master was close by and could see what was going on. When he saw Dick throwing the stones, he jumped up and

A Piece of Bread and a Carrot

caught him by the arm. Then he hit him on the ears so hard that Dick roared with pain and surprise. As soon as we saw the master we ran up closer to see what was going on.

"Bad boy!" he said, "bad boy to chase the colts! This is not the first time but it will be the last. There—take your money and go home. I don't want you on my farm again."

So we never saw Dick again. Old Daniel, the man who looked after the horses, was as gentle as our master, so we were very lucky.

"Bad Boy to Chase the Colts!"

Squire Gordon

Chapter 2
My Breaking In

I was beginning to grow handsome. My coat was fine and soft and deep black. I had one white foot and a pretty white star on my forehead. Everyone was impressed with me, but my master would not sell me until I was four years old. He said that boys should not work like men and colts should not work like full-grown horses.

When I was four years old, Squire Gordon came to look at me. He examined my eyes, mouth and legs. I had to walk, trot and gallop for him. He seemed to like me, and he said:

"After he has been broken in, he will be just fine."

My master said he would break me in himself, since he did not want me to be frightened or hurt. He said he would begin the very next day.

Everyone may not know what breaking in is, so I will describe it. It means to teach a horse to wear a saddle and bridle and to carry a rider on his or her back. The horse must also learn how to behave when pulling a cart. He must go fast or slow, just as the driver wishes. He must never rear up at something he sees, speak to other horses, or bite or kick. A good horse always obeys his master, even if he is tired or hungry. But worst of all, when his harness is on, he may not jump for joy or lie down to rest. So you can see that this breaking in is a very difficult thing.

I had long been used to a halter and a

My Master Will Break Me In.

headstall, but now I was to have a bit and a bridle. My master gave me some oats as usual, and after a good deal of coaxing, he got the bit into my mouth and the bridle in place. It was a horrible thing! It hurt quite a lot. Unless you have had a bit in your mouth you cannot possibly know how it feels. A large piece of cold, hard steel as thick as a man's finger is pushed into the mouth, between the teeth, and over the tongue. The ends come out at the corner of the mouth and are held there by straps which go over the head, under the throat, around the nose, and under the chin. There is no way in the world to get rid of the awful thing.

But I knew my mother always wore a bit when she went out, and all horses wore them when they were grown-up. So with the help of my master's kind words and lots of oats, I finally learned how to wear my bit and bridle.

Master Puts the Bit in My Mouth.

The next thing was the saddle. But this was not really so bad. My master put it on my back very gently while old Daniel held my head. While he tied it on, he patted me and talked to me in a kind voice, and then he fed me oats. He did this every day until I began to look forward to the oats and the saddle.

Finally, one morning my master got on my back and rode me around the meadow on the soft grass. It felt strange, but I was very proud to be able to carry my master.

The next thing was putting on the iron shoes. This was very hard at first. My master went with me to the blacksmith's shop to make sure that I was not hurt or frightened. The blacksmith took each one of my feet in his hand and cut away some of the hoof. It did not hurt me, so I stood still on three legs until he had done them all. Then he took a piece of iron the shape of my foot and clapped

Master Rides Me around the Meadow.

it on. He drove some nails through the shoe and into my hoof. This was so the shoe would stay firmly on my foot. My feet felt very stiff and heavy, but in a while I got used to it.

The next thing my master did was to get me used to a harness. I had to get used to wearing a stiff heavy collar on my neck and a bridle with large side pieces against my eyes. These are called blinkers. When I had them on, I could only see straight in front of me. There was also a small saddle with a stiff strap that went right under my tail. This was called the crupper. I hated the crupper. My long tail had to be doubled up and poked through the strap. It made me want to kick, but I loved my master too much to do such a thing.

Another thing my master did was to let me spend two weeks in a meadow which was close to the railroad tracks. When I first heard and saw a train, I became very

At the Blacksmith's

frightened, and I ran away as fast as I could. But soon I got used to seeing trains.

Since this time, I have seen many horses run or throw their riders at the sight of a train. But thanks to my master's care, I am as fearless at railway stations as I am in my own stable.

My master often drove me in double harness with my mother. She was steady and could teach me many things. She told me the better I behaved the better I would be treated, and it was wise to try to please my master. She also warned me that not all men were kind, and that many people could be mean and foolish. She told me also that a horse has no control over who may buy him. It made me worry to think that someday I might be at the mercy of a cruel or foolish owner.

In Double Harness with My Mother

"Good-Bye, Blackie."

Chapter 3
Birtwick Park

In early May my master sold me to Squire Gordon, who lived in a place called "Birtwick Park." I was sad to leave my owner, but he patted me softly and said, "Good-bye, Blackie."

Squire Gordon had a large country home. The stable where I lived was big enough for four stalls and had a large swinging window which opened into the yard. In my stall, I was never tied up, and I could move around as much as I pleased. This was very important to me. The stall was clean and airy. I could even see over the walls and into the yard.

After I had eaten my first meal in my new home, I looked into the stall next to mine. There stood a fat gray pony with a thick mane and tail, a very pretty head, and a pert little nose.

I put my head up to the wall and said, "How are you and what is your name?"

He turned around and said, "My name is Merrylegs. I am very handsome. I carry the young women on my back, and sometimes I take our mistress out in the low carriage. Everyone likes me. Are you going to live next to me?"

I said, "Yes."

"Well then," he said, "I hope you are good-tempered and do not bite."

Just then another horse's head looked over from another stall. This was a tall chestnut mare whose ears were laid back and whose

Merrylegs

eyes looked angry. She gave me a cruel look and refused to answer me when I spoke to her.

In the afternoon, when she went out, Merrylegs told me all about it. He explained that Ginger got her name because she used to snap at everyone. He told me that Ginger had been treated very badly by her former owners, and because of that she developed a very bad temper. Merrylegs had noticed a slow change in Ginger since she had come to Birtwick Park. John, the groom, had been treating her with a special kindness, and Merrylegs was sure this would improve Ginger's temper.

Merrylegs Tells Me about Ginger.

Blinkers over My Eyes

Chapter 4
Freedom

I was very happy in my new home, but there was one thing I missed—freedom! For over three years I had all the freedom I wanted. But then, week after week, month after month, and year after year, I had to stand up in a stable day and night until I was needed. And even then, I had to stand steady and quiet, with straps here and there, a bit in my mouth, and blinkers over my eyes. All this was uncomfortable for me, but I knew this is how horses must live. But for a young horse full of strength and spirit, who has been used to a large field where he can fling up his head and toss up his tail and gallop away at full speed, it was very hard to get used to standing in a stable day after day.

Sometimes, when I had less exercise than usual, I felt so full of life that when John came to take me out for a run, I could hardly keep steady. But John was always understanding and seemed to know what it must have felt like to be cooped up in a small stable all day. As soon as we were out of the village, he let me run at a good pace for a few miles.

On Sundays the horses were given a few hours of freedom to roam in the fields. This was a great treat for us. The grass was cool and soft for our feet. It was a wonderful feeling to run and gallop as we pleased.

A Few Hours of Freedom

Ginger and I Talk.

Chapter 5
Ginger

One day when Ginger and I were standing alone in the shade we had a chance to talk. She asked me all about my life and my breaking in, and I told her all there was to tell.

"Well," she said, "if I had your experiences, I might have a good temper too. But now I think it is too late for me."

When I asked her why, Ginger told me all about her life.

She had been taken from her mother when she was very young and put with a lot of other young colts. There was no one to care for her, and there was no kind master to look out for her and show her affection. In the field where she used to run, there was a young boy who would throw stones at the colts. Ginger was never hurt, but one of the other colts was hit in the face and scarred for life. When it came time for her breaking in, she was captured by several rough men, who forced the halter and bar into her mouth. When she tried to protest they whipped her until her flanks ached. After that, Ginger was kept in a small dark stall. Her master's son was a cruel drunkard who wanted to break her high spirits. If she did not do exactly as he pleased, he would make her run around the training field until she was so tired she could hardly stand.

One day he worked her so hard that she lay down and felt tired, miserable and angry. The very next morning he came for her early

Throwing Stones at the Colts

and ran her around the track for a long time. He gave her no rest, and when she began to show her weariness, he whipped her with his crop. This was too much for poor Ginger, and she began to kick and rear up as she had never done before. At last, after a terrible struggle, she was able to throw the cruel man to the ground. Then, without looking behind her, she galloped away into the fields. Ginger stayed there for what seemed like a very long time. She became very hungry and thirsty, and the flies swarmed around her in the hot sun.

Finally, as the sun was going down, an old man who was very kind came out to the field and gave her oats and fresh water to drink. He spoke gently to her in a kind and thoughtful way, and she allowed him to lead her back to the stable.

After he brought her to the stable, he washed her wounds with warm water and

Ginger Throws the Cruel Man.

stood by her and stroked her while she rested. He came to see her often, and she was given to another trainer named Job. He was gentle and thoughtful, and Ginger soon learned what was expected of her.

A Gentle and Thoughtful Trainer

Trying to Be Fashionable

Chapter 6
Ginger's Story Continued

The second time Ginger and I were alone together, she told me about her next home.

After she had been broken in, she was bought by a stylish gentleman and sent to the city. Her new master wanted more than anything else to be fashionable. So he pulled her reins very tight. He did this so that Ginger would keep her head held high for hours at a time. He did not want her to move at all. She also had to wear two bits which were so sharp that they hurt her tongue and made it bleed. Sometimes she was made to stand outside a place and wait for her master. If she moved or put her head down, she was whipped. It was enough to drive her mad. When she was miserable and angry she only received a harsh word or a blow. Ginger was willing to work and make her owners proud, but they cared nothing about her and only made her suffer.

The pain in her mouth and her neck became so unbearable that when anyone came to harness her, she would snap and kick.

Finally, Ginger could stand it no more, and she broke out of her harness and ran away. After this she was sold to a few different owners. People were afraid of her bad temper so she did not stay in any home for a very long time. Her last master was very rough and poked Ginger with a pitchfork if she did not obey. One day when he tried to beat her with a riding whip, she bit him on the arm. From that time on, he was afraid to come too

A Rough Master

close to her. So Ginger learned one way for a horse to deal with human cruelty.

But Ginger then told me that since she had been living here at Birtwick, her life had changed in many ways. John and James, the stable grooms, have learned to treat her with a special kindness. I noticed that as the weeks wore on she grew more gentle and cheerful and was beginning to lose the angry look she had when I first met her.

John and James, the Stable Grooms

James Warns Merrylegs to Behave.

Chapter 7
Merrylegs

Mr. Bloomfield was the vicar who lived in the village. He had a large family with many children. When he came to visit, all the children liked to ride on Merrylegs.

One afternoon Merrylegs had been out with them a long time. When James brought him in and put on his halter, he said:

"There now, you had better behave yourself, or we will get into trouble."

"What have you been doing, Merrylegs?" I asked with surprise.

"Oh!" he said tossing his little head, "I

have been giving those children a lesson. They just don't know when they have had enough or when I have had enough, so I threw them off my back. That is the only thing they could understand."

I was very shocked to hear that Merrylegs would do such a thing, but he explained that he was very careful with the children, especially the girls. Whenever they seemed frightened or a little unsteady he would go as smooth as a cat, and when he felt them getting used to things he would speed up. But this time, after he had been ridden for over two hours, the boys wanted to ride some more. They cut whips out of hazel sticks and hit him a little too hard. Merrylegs stopped two or three times to let them know that he was tired. But the boys thought of him as a machine that could go on for as long as they wanted. They never thought of him as a living pony who had feelings and who could get

Merrylegs Is Careful with the Children.

tired and angry. So when the boy who was riding him began to whip him on the legs, Merrylegs just lifted up his hind legs and let the boy slip off. Merrylegs truly loved children, but he thought he had to teach these boys a lesson. Everyone trusted him, and he returned the trust by trying to be as gentle as possible with the children.

After he explained what had happened, he turned to me and said:

"I would never take to kicking or showing a bad temper. If I did, I would be sold in a jiffy, and I might find myself worked to death by a butcher or at some seaside resort where no one cared for me except to find out how fast I could go. Or I might be whipped by cruel men on a Sunday spree. No, I will be very careful so I will never come to that."

Merrylegs Teaches the Boy a Lesson.

Grazing in the Orchard

Chapter 8
A Talk in the Orchard

One warm afternoon we were all let out to graze and talk under the shady trees in the orchard. I stood next to Sir Oliver, who was an old but very handsome horse. I had often wondered why his tail was so short. It was really only six or seven inches long and had a tassel of hair hanging from it. So I took this opportunity to ask him how he lost his tail.

"It was no accident!" he snorted. "It was a cruel and shameful act. When I was very young I was taken to a place where these cruel things were done. I was tied up so that I couldn't move. Then they came and cut off my long and beautiful tail. They cut through the flesh and the bone."

"How horrible!" I said.

"It was horrible, but it was not only the pain that made it so horrible. It was the indignity of having such a beautiful thing taken from me. I need a tail to brush the flies away. I can't tell you how tormenting it is to have those flies settle on my body and sting me, and to have no way to brush them off. I tell you it is a lifelong wrong and a lifelong loss, but thank heaven, they no longer cut off our tails."

"Why did they do it then?" asked Ginger.

"For fashion!" said the old horse with a stamp of his foot. "Fashion means that someone got it into his head the horses must have their tails cut short to look good. If God had wanted us to have short tails, he surely

Bothered by Flies

would have made us that way."

"And I suppose it is fashion that makes them strap our heads with those horrid bits that I was tortured with in the city," said Ginger.

"Of course it is," answered Sir Oliver. "The whole idea of fashion is one of the most wicked things that people ever thought up. For example, look what they do to dogs. They cut off their tails and pin back their ears because they think it makes them look cute. I had a wonderful friend once, a brown terrier. Her name was 'Sky.' She liked me so much that she used to sleep in my stall. She had a litter of five pretty little puppies. She loved them so! One day a man came and took them all away. In the evening poor Sky brought them back again, one by one in her mouth. They were not the happy little puppies I had known. They were bleeding and crying. They all had had a piece of their tails cut off and

Unhappy Little Puppies

the soft flap on their ears was sheared off as well. How their mother licked them, and how troubled she was, poor thing! I never forgot it. They healed in time, and they forgot the pain, but the nice soft flap that was intended to protect the delicate part of their ears from dust and injury was gone forever. Why don't people cut their own children's ears into points or cut the ends off their noses to make them look cute? It would make as much sense as what they do to us."

Sir Oliver was a gentle old fellow, but all this made him very angry. When he told me this I got angry too. I felt bitter towards people. I had never felt this way before, but the stories I just had heard made me wonder why people could be so cruel. Ginger listened to our conversation and flung up her head and flared her nostrils. She declared that men were both brutes and blockheads.

"Who is talking about blockheads?" said

Sky and Her Puppies.

Merrylegs, who just came up from an old apple tree where he had been rubbing himself against a low branch. "Blockhead is a bad word."

"Bad words are made for bad things," said Ginger, and she told him what Sir Oliver had told us.

"It is all true," said Merrylegs, "and I have seen that happen to the dogs many times. But let's not talk about it here. You all know that master, John and James are always good to us. You know that there are good people as well as bad people. So let's be thankful that we are living here and are receiving kind treatment."

This wise speech cooled us all down. Sir Oliver admitted that he was very fond of his masters, and that his life here was good.

So we broke off our conversation and raised our spirits by munching on some sweet apples which lay scattered on the grass.

Merrylegs Comes to Talk to Us.

A Wonderful Name

Chapter 9
A Stormy Day

After I had been in my new home for a little while, my master decided to give me a proper name. He looked at me very carefully and stroked my head. After a short time, he called John and James and asked them what they thought of the name "Black Beauty."

"Black Beauty—why, yes, I think that is a very good name, and it certainly fits him," said John.

It made me feel proud and very grown-up to have such a wonderful name and such a fine home.

Not long after I was given my name, my master needed to take a long business trip. I was to pull the dog cart, and John went with our master. I always liked the dog cart, because it was so light and the high wheels ran along so smoothly. There had been a great deal of rain, and now the wind was very strong, and the dry leaves blew across the road. We went along at a good pace until we came to the wooden bridge.

The man at the gate of the bridge said the river was rising fast. He feared it would be a rough night. Many of the meadows were already under water, and in one low part of the road the water was halfway up to my knees. The master drove gently and was very careful.

When we got to the town I had a good rest. The master's business took a long time, so we did not start for home until late in the afternoon. By this time the wind was very strong,

"The River Is Rising!"

and I heard the master say to John that he had never been out in such a storm. As we went along, loose branches snapped off the trees, and the wind made fierce howling sounds.

"I wish we were out of these woods," said my master.

"Yes, sir," said John. "It would be dangerous if one of these branches came down on us."

The words were scarcely out of his mouth when there was a groan, and a crack, and a splitting sound. Crashing down among the other trees came an oak which had been torn up by the roots. It fell right across the road just in front of us. I was frightened. I stood still and trembled, but I did not turn around or run away.

"That was a close call," said my master. "What shall we do now?"

John answered that since we couldn't drive

A Tree Crashes Down.

around or over the tree, we should go back to the wooden bridge.

So back we went. By the time we got to the bridge it was nearly dark. We could see that the water was already over the middle of the bridge. My master knew that this sometimes happened during floods, so he did not stop. We were going along at a good pace, but the second my feet touched the first part of the bridge, I knew something was wrong. I stopped and would not go ahead.

"Go on, Beauty," said my master. He gave me a touch with the whip, but I refused to move. He gave me a sharp cut, but I still did not move.

"There must be something wrong, sir," said John, and he jumped out of the cart and came over to me. He tried to lead me forward.

"Come on, Beauty, what's the matter?" he asked. Of course I could not tell him, but I did know that the bridge was not safe.

Something Is Wrong with the Bridge.

Just then the man at the gate to the bridge ran out and waved a torch at us.

"Hoy, hoy, stop! Don't go any further!" he shouted.

"What's the matter?" shouted my master.

"The bridge is broken in the middle, and part of it has been washed away. If you try to cross it, you will land in the river," answered the gatekeeper.

"Thank God!" said my master.

"You Beauty!" said John as he took the bridle and gently turned me around.

The sun had set a long time ago, and the wind seemed to have calmed down. It grew darker and darker. The woods had an eerie stillness. I trotted along quietly, the wheels hardly making a sound on the soft dirt road. Master and John spoke in quiet voices. They realized that by refusing to cross the bridge I had saved their lives. Master said that although people had the power to reason,

"Stop! Stop! The Bridge Is Broken!"

animals had a special knowledge all their own, and this knowledge often saved the lives of the ones they loved. John agreed and passed the night telling many stories of how dogs and horses came to the rescue of their owners. He and master agreed that people did not value their animals half as much as they should.

At last we came to the gates of Birtwick Park. The gardener was standing watch for us. He said that mistress had been up all night worrying about us.

Just then we saw a light at the hall door, and mistress came running out of the house.

"Are you really safe, my dear? Oh! I have been so worried. Did you have an accident?" she asked.

"No, my dear, but if it had not been for Black Beauty we would all have been carried away by the river," answered master.

I heard no more, since they went into the

Mistress Runs Out to Us.

house and John took me to the stable. He gave me a wonderful supper that night and prepared a thick bed of straw. I was truly thankful. It had been a long night and I was very tired.

The Long Night Is Over.

Master Wants to Know about James.

Chapter 10
James Howard

Early one morning in December, John had just led me into the stable after my daily exercise when the master came into the stable. He looked very serious and held an open letter in his hand.

"Good morning, John," said the master. "I want to know if you have any complaints about James."

"No, sir," answered John. "He is a good worker and is fair and gentle with the horses."

The master stood and listened to John.

When John finished talking, the master smiled and looked at James, who was standing in the doorway.

"James, my lad, I asked John about you because I have some news that concerns your future," said the master. "I have here a letter from my brother-in-law. He wants me to find him a trustworthy young groom who knows his business well. My brother-in-law is a good man, and if you could get this job it would be a good start for you. I hate to lose you, especially since I know what a great help you are to John, but this is a fine opportunity and we won't stand in your way. Why don't you think it over and talk about it with your family? Let me know what you have decided."

A few days after this conversation it was decided that James would leave us to go on to this better job. In the meantime, he was to get all the practice in driving that could be given to him. I never saw the carriage go out

A Fine Opportunity for James

so often. Ginger and I were put on the carriage, and James drove us.

We went to many different places in the city. It was a joy for me to see all the other horses and carriages and to smell the scents of bread and tobacco coming from the open shops. In the meantime, James was improving his skills, and Ginger and I were thoroughly enjoying ourselves.

Ginger and I in the City

Long, Heavy Hills

Chapter 11
The Fire

One sunny afternoon, my master and mistress decided to visit some friends who lived about forty-five miles away. The first day James drove the carriage for thirty-two miles. There were long, heavy hills, but James drove so thoughtfully that we did not get very tired. He never forgot to put on the brake as we went downhill, or to take it off at the right place.

We stopped once or twice on the road, and just as the sun was going down we reached the town where we were to spend the night.

We stopped at the inn, which was in the center of the marketplace. It was a very large inn, and we drove under an archway into a long yard. At the end of the yard were the stables and coach houses. Two men came to meet us. One of them patted me on the head and led me to a stable. James stood by as we were rubbed down and cleaned.

Much later in the evening, as I was resting in my stall, I heard a horse being led into the stable. As the horse was being cleaned, a young man with a pipe in his mouth lounged in the stable to talk with the grooms. After a few minutes the groom asked the young man to put out his pipe and pitch some hay into the horse's rack. I heard the man step by me as he threw down the hay. Then the door was locked, and we were left for the night.

I don't know how long I slept or what time of night it was, but I woke up feeling very uncomfortable. The air seemed thick, and I

A Young Man with a Pipe

could hardly breathe. I heard Ginger coughing, and one of the other horses seemed restless. It was very dark, and I could not see a thing, but the stable seemed to be full of smoke.

The trap door had been left open, and I could hear a soft rushing sort of noise and a low crackling and snapping. I began to tremble all over. The other horses were all awake. Some of them were pulling at their halters, and others were stamping at the floor.

At last I heard someone coming. The groom who had brought the last horse in burst into the stable with a lantern. He began to untie the horses and try to lead them out. But he seemed in such a hurry and so frightened himself that he frightened me even more. The first horse would not go with him, so he tried a second and a third. They too would not leave with him. He came to me and tried to drag me out of the stall, but of course I

Bursting into the Stable

wouldn't go with him. After he tried all the horses, he gave up and left the stable.

Maybe we were very foolish not to leave, but we had no idea what was happening, and there was no one around whom we could trust. The fresh air that had come in through the open door made it easier to breathe, but the rushing sound overhead grew louder, and I could see a red light flickering on the wall.

I heard someone outside cry, "Fire!" Then I heard James' voice, quiet and cheery, as it always was:

"Come, my beauties, it is time for us to be off, so wake up and come along."

I stood closest to the door, so he came to me first and patted me on the nose.

"Come, Beauty, on with your bridle, and we'll soon be out of all this," he said as he led me out of the flaming stable.

Once we were out of danger and safe in the yard, he had someone watch me while he

"Fire! Fire!"

went back in to get Ginger. I let out a shrill whinny as I saw him go. Later, Ginger told me that that was the best thing I could have done for her. For when she heard me in the yard she had the courage to leave the stable.

There was a great deal of confusion in the yard. Horses were being led out of other stables, and people were rushing around and shouting. I kept looking at the stable door, where the smoke poured out thicker than ever. Soon I heard my master's voice call out loudly:

"James Howard! James Howard! Are you in there?" There was no answer, but I could hear a crash of something falling in the fire. The next moment I gave a loud, joyful neigh, for I saw James come out through the smoke. He was leading Ginger. She was coughing a lot, and he was not able to speak.

"My brave lad!" said master as he touched James' shoulder. "Are you all right?"

James Leads Ginger Out.

James nodded his head, but he was still unable to speak.

We left the town that same night. Everyone was quite upset. James said that the roof and floor of the stable had fallen in. The horses that could not be led out were buried under the burnt rafters and tiles.

We Leave at Once.

A Kind Coachman Makes Us Comfortable.

Chapter 12
James Leaves Birtwick Park

After the fire, the rest of our journey was very easy. Just before sunset, we reached our destination and were taken into a clean, snug stable. There was a kind coachman who made us very comfortable and who seemed to think a great deal of James when he heard about the fire.

"There is one thing that is quite clear, young man," he said. "Your horses know whom they can trust. It is one of the hardest things in the world to get horses out of a stable when there is a fire or a flood."

We stayed at this place for three days and then returned home. All went well on this journey, and we were glad to be in our own stable again. John was overjoyed to see us all safe and sound.

Before John and James left us for the night, they discussed a young boy named Joe Green. Joe Green was to take James' place when he left Birtwick Park. We heard John say that although Joe was only fourteen years old, he was very bright and willing to learn.

The next day we got our first look at Joe Green. He came to the stables to learn all he could before James left. He learned how to sweep the stable and how to bring in the straw and hay. He was too short to groom either Ginger or me, so James taught him on Merrylegs. Merrylegs did not like this at all and complained about being groomed by a "child who knew nothing." But by the end of

Joe Green

the second week, he confessed that Joe Green was learning well and would turn out all right.

At last the day came when James had to leave us. He looked quite unhappy, although he did his best to try and cover it up. We heard him tell John that he would miss his friends and his family as well as the horses he had come to love so much. But John cheered him up by explaining that he would be sure to make friends in his new home, and that this new job would make his family very proud of him.

Everyone was very sorry to lose James. Merrylegs moped about for several days and even stopped eating. John took him out mornings and let him trot and gallop in the fields until his disposition improved. Still, it was hard to think that we would never see our friend James again. He was a good man who treated us with a special kindness.

James Is Unhappy to Leave.

"Run as Fast as You Can!"

Chapter 13
Going for the Doctor

One night after James had left, I was lying down in the straw fast asleep when I was suddenly awakened by a loud bell. I heard the door of John's house open as he ran up the hall. He was back in a few minutes. He unlocked the stable door and cried:

"Wake up, Beauty! You will have to run as fast as you can!"

Before I knew what was happening, he had the saddle on my back and the bridle on my head. He threw on his coat and took me to the hall door. The butler was standing there with a lamp in his hand.

"Now, John," he said, "ride as fast as you can. Our mistress' life depends upon it. There is not a moment to lose. Give this note to Dr. White and be sure to rest the horse at the inn. Return as soon as you can."

When we reached the road, John said softly:

"Black Beauty, do your best. We must try to save our mistress' life."

After I heard this, I did not need the whip or the spur. I galloped as fast as I could for two miles. When we came to the bridge, John pulled me up a little and patted my neck. "Well done, Beauty," he said. He would have let me go slower, but my spirit was up, and I was off again as fast as before.

It was three in the morning as we arrived at Dr. White's house. John rang the bell twice and then pounded on the door. Finally Dr. White threw open the window and asked

Galloping as Fast as I Can

John what he wanted. After John explained that our mistress was very ill and needed him immediately, he told us to wait there until he came down.

In a few minutes the doctor was at the door, and John handed him the note. Doctor White then explained that his own horse was ill and asked if he could ride back with me. John knew I was overheated and tired, but he realized how important it was for the doctor to reach our mistress.

I will not describe the ride back home. The doctor was an elderly man and not a very good rider. But I did my best, and we soon reached Birtwick Park. Joe was waiting for us at the gate. My master led the doctor into the house, and Joe walked me to the stable. I was glad to be home. My legs were shaking, and I could only stand and pant. I was soaking wet, and my whole body was steaming. Joe rubbed my legs and chest, but he did not put my warm

The Doctor Comes to the Door.

cloth on me. He thought I was too hot and would not like it. He gave me some cold water and some hay and corn. He thought he had done all the right things, and he closed the stable door as he left me for the night. Soon I began to shake and tremble. I got very cold. My legs and chest ached, and I felt sore all over. Oh, how I wished I had my warm blanket. I wished John was at my side, but he still was walking home from the doctor's house, so I lay down in the straw and tried to sleep.

After a long while, I heard John at the door. I gave a low moan, for I was in great pain. He was at my side in a moment. I could not tell him how I felt, but he seemed to know anyway. He covered me up with two or three warm blankets and then ran to the house for some hot water. I heard him complain under his breath about Joe Green. He called him a stupid boy for not covering me

I Lie Down in the Straw.

or giving me something warm to eat and drink.

I was very ill. A strong inflammation had attacked my lungs, and I could not breathe without pain. John nursed me day and night. My master came to see me many times.

"My poor Beauty," he said one day. "You saved your mistress' life, and now you are the one who is so sick."

It made me feel proud that I had saved her life, and I heard John say that he had never seen a horse run so fast in his whole life.

After what seemed like a long time, I began to feel better. The horse doctor came to see me several times, and his medicine helped the fever and inflammation to go away.

John was very angry at Joe Green for quite a while, but he finally came to see that the boy hadn't meant me any harm. He simply had not known any better.

The Horse Doctor Comes.

The Doctor and Master Look Worried.

Chapter 14
Leaving Home

I had lived in Birtwick Park for three happy years, but I felt that something very sad would be happening soon. We heard from time to time that our mistress was ill. The doctor came to the house several times a week, and our master looked grave and worried. Then we heard that our mistress must leave home at once and move to a warm climate for a few years. The news fell upon the household like the tolling of a death bell. Everyone was unhappy, and the master began to make the arrangements for the move. Everything had to be done quickly.

John went about his work, but hardly talked or smiled, and Joe was silent. We soon learned where we would be going next. Master had sold Ginger and me to an old friend who he felt would give us a good home. He gave Merrylegs to the local priest, who had wanted a pony, but he did it only on the condition that Merrylegs would never be sold, and when he couldn't work any longer he would be shot and buried.

When the last sad day came, Ginger and I brought the carriage up to the hall door for the final time. The servants brought out rugs and many other household things. When everything was arranged, master came down the steps carrying mistress in his arms. He said good-bye to each of the servants and thanked them all for their loyalty.

We rode slowly to the railroad station. When we finally got there, mistress said:

Merrylegs Goes to the Priest.

"Good-bye, John. We shall never forget you. God bless you always."

I felt the rein twitch, but John did not answer; perhaps he could not speak. As soon as Joe had taken the things out of the carriage, John called him to stand by the horses while he went on the platform. Poor Joe! He stood close to our heads to hide the tears. Very soon the train came puffing up to the station. In a few minutes the doors closed, the guard whistled, and the train glided away, leaving behind clouds of white smoke and our heavy hearts.

When the train was out of sight, John came back.

"We will never see them again—never," he said. He took the reins, and with Joe alongside him, he drove slowly home. But it was not our home now.

Poor Joe!

Mr. York

Chapter 15
Our New Home

The next morning after breakfast, Joe came to say good-bye to us, and Merrylegs neighed to us from the yard. Then John put the saddle on Ginger and the leading rein on me, and rode us across the county to Earlshall Park, our new home.

After we arrived, John asked for Mr. York, and we waited a long time for him to come outside and meet with us. He was a fine-looking man with a stern voice. He was very friendly and polite to John and looked us over quickly before he called a groom to take us to the stable.

We were taken to a light, airy stable and placed in stalls adjoining each other. In about half an hour John and Mr. York came in to see us. Mr. York asked John to tell him about any particular habits or likes and dislikes that Ginger or I might have. John explained that we were a good team and could be expected to work hard if treated well and with kindness. He told Mr. York of Ginger's hard life and warned that if she was treated badly she would return to her bad-tempered ways.

They were going out of the stable when John stopped and said, "I had better tell you that we have never used the check-rein with either of them. The black horse never has had one on, and the dealer said it was the gag-bit that spoiled Ginger's temper."

"Well," said York, "if they come here they must wear the check-rein. I prefer a loose

A New Stable

rein myself, and the owner is very understanding about horses. But his wife has other ideas. She wants to be fashionable, and she demands that the horses be reined tightly whenever she goes out in the carriage."

"I am very sorry about this," said John, "but please try to treat the horses with kindness, for they are used to good treatment."

Then he came around to us and spoke to us in a soft and loving voice. He sounded very sad.

I held my face close to him. That was the only way I could say good-bye. Before I knew it he was gone, and I never saw him again.

The next day our new owner came to see us. He seemed quite pleased with us and listened thoughtfully while Mr. York repeated what John had told him about the check-rein. Our new master said he understood, but that his wife insisted upon using this tight rein. He told Mr. York to be gentle with us and to

John Says Good-Bye.

get us used to the rein a little at a time.

The next day we were harnessed and put on the carriage. The mistress came to look at us. She was a tall, elegant-looking woman, but something was bothering her. She said nothing and got into the carriage. This was my first time wearing the check-rein, and although it was uncomfortable not to be able to get my head down once in a while, it did not pull my head higher than I was used to. I was a little worried about Ginger, but she seemed to be quiet and content.

The next afternoon, we were again put on the carriage, and our mistress came down to meet us.

"Mr. York," she said, "you must put those horses' heads higher. I don't like the way they look."

York explained that we were not used to a tight rein, but the mistress still asked him to tighten the rein.

Our New Mistress

Soon I began to understand all the stories I had heard from the other horses. Day by day, hole by hole, our bearing reins were shortened, and instead of looking forward to having the harness put on, as I used to, I began to dread it. When we pulled the carriage uphill, I had to pull with my head up. That took all the spirit out of me. My back and my legs ached with pain. Ginger too seemed restless, but she said very little.

At last I thought the worst was over, since for several days there was no more shortening. But I was soon to learn that the worst was yet to come.

Driving with a Check-Rein

Ginger Rears Up.

Chapter 16
Rebellion

One afternoon, our mistress came down later than usual to take her daily ride. She looked angry and ordered York to raise our heads up even higher. York came to me first. He drew my head back and fixed the rein so tight that it was almost unbearable. Then he went to Ginger, who was jerking her head up and down against the bit. She had a good idea what was coming, and the second York took the rein off in order to shorten it she reared up so suddenly that York was hit in the nose and the groom was nearly knocked over. At once they both tried to calm her, but she was a match for them and went on plunging, rearing and kicking. At last she kicked right over the carriage pole and fell down. There is no telling what else she might have done if York had not held her head down to stop her from struggling.

The groom soon set me free from Ginger and the carriage and led me back to the stable. Before long, Ginger was led in by two other grooms. She had been knocked around and bruised. York came with her and looked us both over. He seemed very upset and complained about a world that cared more for fashion than living things. He was sorry that he hadn't taken a stronger stand when the mistress insisted that our reins be made shorter.

Ginger was never put on the carriage again, but as soon as her bruises healed, one of the master's sons said he would like to have her, for he was sure she would make a

Trying to Calm Ginger

good hunter. I still was used to pull the carriage. Only this time I had a new partner.

What I suffered with that rein for four long months would be hard to describe. I am sure that if it had lasted much longer, my health and temper both would have given way. I would foam at the mouth because of the sharp bit on my tongue and jaw and the unnatural position of my head. There was also a terrible pressure on my windpipe which made my breathing very uncomfortable. When I returned to the stable my mouth and tongue ached, and my neck and chest were sore. I also felt worn and depressed.

In my old home I always knew that John and my master were my friends, but here I had no friends. York surely must have known how the rein hurt me, but he did nothing.

Sore and Aching

Reuben Smith Is Left in Charge.

Chapter 17
Reuben Smith

When York went away on business, a man named Reuben Smith was left in charge of the stables. He was a gentle and clever man, and he knew how to care for horses. But Reuben Smith had one problem—he drank too much. He did not drink all the time. He could be steady for weeks or months, but then he would break loose and get very drunk. At these times he was a disgrace to himself, a terror to his wife, and a nuisance to everyone around him. York knew about Reuben's problem, but they had talked it over, and Reuben promised that he would not touch another drop of alcohol as long as he worked at the stable. York trusted him, and so he thought Reuben could be trusted to fill his place while he was away.

It was now early in April and the family was expected home some time in May. I was chosen to pull the carriage to town to run some errands. Reuben drove the carriage at a steady pace. When we reached the town, I was sent to a stable to be fed and rested. A nail in one of my front shoes had come loose, but the stable groom did not notice it. After a few hours, Reuben returned. He said we would not be going home for another hour, since he had met some old friends and wanted to spend some time with them. By this time, the groom had noticed the loose nail in my shoe and asked Reuben if he should do something about it.

"No," said Reuben, "that will be all right

A Loose Nail

until we get home."

He spoke in a very loud, offhand way, and I thought it was unlike him not to see about the shoe, since he was usually so careful and concerned about these things. He also seemed to be in a bad mood and had a sour expression on his face.

He finally returned about nine o'clock in the evening. It was obvious that he had been drinking. We started out on the journey home while it was still very dark. Before we were out of the town, Reuben began to lead me in a fast gallop. The roads were very stony, and at this fast pace, my shoe became so loose that it fell off. If Reuben had not been drunk, he would have noticed this right away. But instead, he urged me to go faster and faster until my foot began to ache terribly. The hoof broke and split down to the quick, and the inside was badly cut from the sharp stones.

I could not go on. The pain was just too

Reuben Urges Me Faster.

much to bear. I stumbled and fell with great force on both my knees. Reuben fell off my back, and since we were going so fast, he fell with a loud thud, for I thought I could hear his body hit the ground. I soon recovered my balance and limped to the side of the road. The moon had just risen, and I could see Reuben lying a few yards away. He did not move, but I could hear him groaning. I stood there by the road in great pain. It was a calm April night, and it made me think of the summer nights long ago, when I used to lie beside my mother in the green, pleasant meadow.

As the pain grew worse, I listened for the sound of footsteps, or horses or wheels. I hoped someone would come soon to help us.

Reuben Does Not Move.

"He's Dead."

Chapter 18
How It Ended

It must have been almost midnight when I finally heard the sound of horses' feet. As the sound came nearer and nearer I was sure I could hear Ginger's step. As soon as I was positive it was her, I neighed loudly. The carriage came slowly over the stones and stopped at the dark, motionless figure that lay upon the ground.

One of the men jumped down and held up Reuben's limp arm.

"He's dead," he said. "Feel how cold his hands are."

They lifted him up, but there was no life. His hair was soaked with blood. When they laid him down again, they looked at me. They noticed my cut knees and my bad foot. The two men soon figured out what had happened. They realized that Reuben had caused his own death by drinking too much.

After they talked for a while, we began the slow, sad journey home. I limped and hobbled with great pain. At last I reached the stable, and my knees were wrapped in wet cloths and my foot was tied up with medication. I managed to lie down in the soft straw and sleep in spite of the great pain.

The next day the horse doctor came and examined my legs. He said that he hoped I would not be spoiled by the fall, but even so, I would never lose the scars on my knees. They did their best to cure me, but it took a long time and was very painful. Scar tissue came up in my knees, and it was burned out

Noticing the Cut Knees

with an ointment. When at last it was healed, they put a blistering fluid on the front of both knees to take all the hair off. They had some reason for this, and I suppose they knew what they were doing.

Since Reuben's death was so sudden and there were no witnesses, an inquest was held. The innkeeper testified that Reuben had been very drunk when he left town that night and was riding at a fast gallop. My shoe was picked up among the stones, so the cause of death was quite clear and I was cleared of all blame.

The Cause of Death

Alone in the Meadow

Chapter 19
Ruined and Going Downhill

As soon as my knees healed, I was turned out to a small meadow for a month or two. No other animals were there, and although I enjoyed the freedom and the sweet grass, I was very lonely. Ginger and I had become good friends, and now I missed her a great deal. I often neighed when I heard horses passing on the road, but I rarely got an answer. Then one morning the gate was opened, and Ginger trotted towards me. I whinnied joyfully and ran to meet her. But I soon found that she had not been sent to the meadow just to keep me company. Her story would be too long to tell, but it ended with her being ruined by hard riding. Now she had been sent here to see what rest and some freedom would do for her.

Ginger looked at me sadly and said, "Here we are, ruined in the prime of our youth and strength. Life is very hard for us."

We both felt that we were not what we had been. However, that did not spoil the pleasure we had in each other's company. We did not gallop about as we once did, but we fed on the sweet grass and stood under one of the shady lime trees with our heads close to each other.

One day we saw our master come into the meadow. He had just returned from a long trip. York was with him, and they examined us carefully. Our master was very upset.

"These horses were given to me by my friend, who thought they would find a good

Together Again

home with me. Now they have been ruined. Ginger should stay here for a few months and then we'll see what she'll be like. But the black one must be sold. It is too bad, but I cannot have knees like that in my stable."

York urged our master to sell me to a man he knew who would treat me well and would not mind my appearance.

So I was sent by train to another town. When I reached the end of my journey, I found myself in a comfortable stable, but it was not airy or large. My new owner kept many horses and carriages which he rented out by the day. Sometimes his own men drove, and other times the horse and carriage were rented to ladies and gentlemen who drove themselves.

Before this time, I always had been driven by people who at least knew how to drive. But in this place I was driven by all sorts of people. One time, I was rented by a man and

I Am Sent by Train.

his family. He flopped the reins as we started and of course gave me several cuts with the whip, even though I was keeping up a good pace. There were a great many loose stones in the road, and I got a stone stuck in my front hoof. A good driver would have noticed that something was wrong after I had gone two or three paces. This man was so busy laughing and talking that he noticed nothing. After we went over half a mile, he finally became aware that I was lame. A friendly farmer stopped us on the road and removed the stone from my aching hoof. Experiences such as this were common to me while I was hired out as a job horse.

After a few months of this rough treatment, I was rented to a gentleman who clearly knew how to drive a horse. He seemed pleased with me, and I arched my neck and set off at my best pace. It seemed like old times again, and it made me feel quite happy.

Rough Treatment

This gentleman took a great liking to me, and after trying me several times with the saddle he asked my master to sell me to a friend of his who wanted a safe, good-natured horse for riding. And so it came to pass that I was sold to Mr. Barry that summer.

I Am Sold to Mr. Barry.

Filcher, My Groom

Chapter 20
A Thief

My new master lived alone in a small house. He was a businessman, and his doctor told him that horseback riding would be good for his health. He rented a stable near the house and hired a man named Filcher as my groom. My master knew very little about horses, but he treated me well. He ordered the best hay with plenty of oats, crushed beans and bran. I heard the master order this food, and I thought I was well off.

For a few days everything was fine. The groom kept the stable clean, and he washed and brushed me. After a while I noticed that my food was not just right. I had beans and bran, but there were not many oats. In two or three weeks this began to show. I became weak and depressed, but there was no way I could tell anyone what was happening to me. This went on for months, and I wondered why my master did not notice that something was wrong. One afternoon he rode out into the country to see a friend of his. This friend knew a great deal about horses. After he welcomed his friend, he looked at me and said:

"It seems to me that your horse does not look too well. I hate to say anything, but it looks as though he has not been eating properly."

My master explained that he had ordered the best food for me. Both men thought for a moment, and then my master realized that something was happening to my food.

If I could have spoken I would have told

"Your Horse Does Not Look Well."

my master where my oats went. My groom used to come every morning with a little boy who carried a covered basket. They would go into the harness-room and fill a little bag with my oats, and then the boy would go home.

Five or six days after our visit with my master's friend, just as the boy left the stable, the door was pushed open and a policeman stood holding the child by the arm. The boy looked frightened and tried to call out. The policeman made him show them where the oats were kept and how he filled up his basket every morning.

They soon found Filcher and brought both him and the boy to prison. I heard later that the boy was released, but Filcher was locked up for two months.

The Thief

Swollen, Infected Hooves

Chapter 21
A Horse Fair

After this experience with Filcher, my master hired a new groom. On the surface he seemed like a good enough fellow who liked horses. But as the days went by, he began to neglect my care. He rarely exercised me, and he went for weeks without cleaning my stable. After a while, I developed a bad infection in my hooves from standing in a damp and dirty stable.

Mr. Barry was so disgusted with the behavior of his two grooms that he decided it was too much trouble to keep a horse.

A few days later I found myself up for sale at a horse fair. A horse fair may be fun for people, but it is very serious business for a horse. I was put with two or three other strong, useful-looking horses, and a good many people came to look at us.

The first thing they did was to pull my mouth open, then to look at my eyes, then feel all the way down my legs, and give me a hard feel of the skin and flesh. Some people did this in a rough, careless way, and others would take care to pat me gently and talk to me in a soft voice.

There was one man I hoped would buy me. He was small and well built. His eyes were a soft gray, and he spoke to me in a kind and gentle voice.

He offered a good price for me but it was refused. I looked after him, but he was gone. Next, a hard-looking man with a loud voice came. I was very afraid he would buy me, but

The Horse Fair

luckily he walked away. One or two men came by, but they did not make an offer. Then the hard-faced man came back and began to bargain for me. Just then the gray-eyed man returned. I reached my head out towards him. He stroked my nose and offered the salesman more money than the hard-faced man.

The money was paid on the spot, and my new master took my halter and led me out of the fair. He fed me oats and stood by while I ate. He talked to me for a while; then we started on our way home.

After a long ride, my owner pulled up at a small house and whistled. The door flew open, and a young woman followed by a little girl and boy ran out. There was a lively greeting as my rider dismounted.

The next minute they were all standing around patting me and talking to me in sweet voices. It felt good to be in this place!

A Warm Welcome

Polly

Chapter 22
A City Cab Horse

My new master's name was Jeremiah Baker, but everyone called him Jerry. His wife's name was Polly, and she was a handsome woman with smooth, dark hair, dark eyes, and a merry little mouth. They had two children, a boy of twelve, and a girl named Dolly who was eight. They all loved each other very much, and I had never seen such a happy family before. Jerry drove a cab in the city. I was to pull the carriage with his other horse, who was named Captain.

On the first morning in my new home, I

was visited by Polly and Dolly. They seemed eager to get to know me and to make friends. It was a great treat to be petted and talked to again. They brought me little apples and pieces of bread. They both thought I was very handsome and wondered how my knees had been so badly damaged.

In the afternoon I was put into the cab for the first time. Jerry was very careful to see that the collar and bridle fitted comfortably. There was no check-rein and no need to stand with my head held too high. Jerry was proud of me and showed me off to the other cab drivers. Many of them thought that there must be something wrong with me since I was such a fine-looking horse. But Jerry only smiled and stroked my neck.

The first week of pulling the cab was very hard for me. I was not used to the city noise and traffic. But I soon found that I could trust Jerry, and I slowly got used to all the

Polly and Dolly Make Friends.

confusion and the busy streets.

In a very short time Jerry and I understood each other as well as horse and man can. He made the stables as comfortable as possible and fed Captain and me very well. But the best thing about being a cab horse was having our Sunday rest. Captain and I worked so hard during the week that Sunday was a special time for us. We had a chance to relax and to enjoy each other's company. In a short time we became good friends, and I learned all about my new stable mate. Our friendship grew, and I soon came to love my new home and feel like my old self again.

Sunday Rest

Two Men Come Out of a Tavern.

Chapter 23
Jerry Barker

I never knew a better man than my new master. He was kind and good, and always stood up for what he believed in. He was so good tempered that very few people could pick a quarrel with him. Jerry could not bear wasting time, and the one thing that could make him angry was people who wanted him to whip the horses to run faster, so that they would not be late for an appointment.

One afternoon, two wild-looking young men came out of a tavern and called to Jerry:

"Here cabby! Look sharp, we are late. If

you get us to the station in time for the one o'clock train we'll reward you well."

Jerry explained that he would take them at a safe pace, and he would ask only for the regular fare. The men thought for a moment and decided to give Jerry a chance.

It is always difficult to drive fast in a city in the middle of the day when the streets are full of traffic. But when a good driver and a good horse work together, it is amazing what they can do. Jerry and I were used to the busy, crowded streets, and no one could top us at getting through when we set our minds on it. Although things were jammed up that particular day, Jerry and I wove skillfully through the traffic and arrived at the station with five minutes to spare. Our passengers were quite happy and relieved that they had made their train.

"Thank God we are on time," said one of the men, "and thank you, too, my friend and

Weaving through the Traffic

your good horse. You have saved us more than money can pay for."

The young man offered Jerry extra money, but my master remained true to his word and refused it. He helped the young men with their baggage and watched as they disappeared into the crowded station. It was a good feeling to know that we had used our skills to help these two young men. Jerry wondered out loud what could have been so important about that particular train.

That evening, as Jerry brushed me and gave me some warm oats, he told Dolly and Polly about our ride through the city traffic. They laughed when they began to think of why the young men were in such a hurry. But they were serious when they patted my head and thanked me for getting Jerry and the passengers to the station safely.

The Men Go into the Station.

A Poor Hungry Creature

Chapter 24
Poor Ginger

One day, while our cab and many others were waiting outside one of the parks, a shabby old cab drove up beside ours. The horse was an old worn-out chestnut, with an ill-kept coat and bones that showed plainly through it. Her knees knuckled over, and her forelegs were very unsteady. I had been eating some hay, and the wind rolled a little of it toward her. The poor creature put out her long, thin neck and picked it up, and then turned and looked around for more. There was a hopeless look in a dull eye that I could not help noticing. I was thinking that I had seen that horse before, when she looked at me and said, "Black Beauty, is that you?"

It was Ginger! But she was so different! The beautifully arched and glossy neck was now straight and sunken in. Her clean straight legs were swollen, and the joints were grown out of shape with hard work. Her face was full of suffering and pain.

She came close to me and told me her sad story.

After a twelve-month run in the field where I had last seen her, she was considered to be fit for work again and was sold to a new master. For a little while she got on very well, but after a longer gallop than usual, the old strain returned. After a short rest, she was sold again. She had a few more owners, and finally she was sold to a man who kept cabs and horses and rented them out.

"When they found out my weakness they

Poor Ginger

said I was not worth what they paid for me and that I must go on one of the small cabs and just be used up. And that is what they are doing. They whip me and work me, without ever thinking of what I am feeling. I never even get a Sunday rest," she said sadly.

"But you used to stand up for yourself when you were badly treated," I said.

"Ah!" she said. "I did once, but it's no use. Men are stronger, and if they are cruel and have no feelings there is nothing that we can do. I suppose we can only bear it—bear it on and on until we are dead. I wish I was dead now, so that I would not have to suffer another day of this terrible life."

I was very upset and sad beyond words. I put my nose up to hers, but I could say nothing to comfort her. I think she was happy to see me, for she said:

"You are the only friend I ever had."

I Put My Nose up to Ginger.

Just then her driver came up, and with a tug at her mouth, he backed her out of the cab line and drove off.

A short time after this a cart with a dead horse in it passed our cab-stand. The head hung out of the cart, and the lifeless tongue was slowly dripping blood. The sight was horrible! It was a chestnut horse with a long, thin neck. I saw a white streak down the forehead. I think it was Ginger. In a way I hoped it was, for then her troubles would be over. Oh, if people were really kind, they would shoot us before we came to such misery.

Ginger's Troubles Are Over.

Waiting for Hours

Chapter 25
Jerry's New Year

For some people holidays like Christmas and the New Year are very happy times, but this is not true for cab drivers and their horses. There are so many parties that the work is hard and goes on late into the night. Sometimes a driver and horse have to wait for hours in the rain or frost, shivering with cold, while the lucky people are inside dancing and celebrating.

We had a great deal of work in the Christmas week, and Jerry had a bad cough. But no matter how late we were, Polly would sit up for us and come out to meet us with a lantern. Many times she looked worried and expressed her fears about Jerry's health.

On the evening of the New Year we had to take two gentlemen to a house in one of the city squares. We dropped them off at nine o'clock, and they told us to return again at eleven. They added that since it was a party they might be a few minutes late, but that we should wait anyway.

As the clock struck eleven we were at the door. The clock chimed every ten minutes until it was twelve o'clock, but still the door did not open.

The wind had been very changeable, and now it blew cold, hard sleet in our faces. Jerry got off the cab and pulled one of my blankets up further on my neck. By this time Jerry was coughing badly, and there was no shelter from the cold winds and driving rain and sleet.

Jerry Pulls Up My Blanket.

At a quarter after one the door opened and the two gentlemen came out. They got into the cab without a word and told Jerry where to drive. My legs were numb with cold, and I was afraid I might fall. When the men got out they never even said they were sorry for having kept us waiting for so long. They were angry at having to pay Jerry for waiting for them.

At last we got home. Jerry could hardly speak, and his cough was worse than ever. Polly did not say a thing, but her face showed her concern. As tired as he was, Jerry fed me some warm food and gave me a good rubdown.

It was late the next morning before anyone came to the stable. Jerry's son came and cleaned and fed us. He was very still and I could sense that something was wrong. Later in the day Polly came over to the stable. I could hear her talking to her children. She

The Gentlemen Finally Come Out.

was crying, and I could gather from what they said that Jerry was dangerously ill.

For three days, we waited for news. It seemed there was a chance that Jerry might die. After a week, I heard Polly announce that Jerry had passed the danger point.

Jerry grew better slowly, but the doctor said that he must never go back to the cab work again. The children talked a lot about what their parents would do and how they could help them.

Very soon after Jerry's health began to improve, he received a letter from an old friend. She was an elderly widow who lived in the country. She wrote to tell Jerry and Polly about an empty cottage that the family could have. It was right near her own home, and she could offer Jerry work as a coachman. There was also a good school nearby for the children.

It was quickly decided that as soon as

Polly Talks to Her Children.

Jerry was well enough they should move to the country, and that the cab and horses should be sold as soon as possible.

This was sad news for me, for I was no longer young and could not look for any improvement in my health. I loved my master and my home, and even though my work was hard, I did it well.

Jerry said I should not be sold for cab work, and entrusted his good friend to find a new home for me.

The time finally came for leaving. Jerry was not yet allowed out of bed, so I never saw him again. Polly and the children came to say good-bye. Polly talked softly to me and said that she wished they could take me with them. And then laying her hand on my mane, she put her face close to my neck and kissed me. I could still feel her soft touch as I was led away to my new place.

Good-Bye Again

Loading the Wagon with Grain

Chapter 26
Jakes and the Old Woman

I was sold to a corn dealer and baker. Jerry knew the man, and he was sure I would have good work and a comfortable home. He would have been right, except that my new owner was not always around to supervise his workers. There was a foreman at the stable who was always hurrying about and driving everyone to work harder and faster. Many times he loaded me up with more goods than I could pull comfortably. My driver, whose name was Jakes, often told the foreman that I was carrying a load that was too heavy. But since Jakes was only a worker, the foreman ignored his advice.

In this new job, I wore a check-rein again, and after four months of carrying those heavy loads, my strength began to fail. One day I was loaded up more than usual, and part of the road was a steep uphill climb. I used all my strength, but I could hardly move, and I had to stop. Jakes became quite angry and started shouting at me.

"Get on, you lazy fellow, or I shall whip you!" he shouted.

He began hitting me again and again with the whip. The sharp leather dug into my flesh and just as it seemed like I could not stand it for another minute, I heard a woman's voice say:

"Oh, please do not whip your good horse any more. I am sure he is doing all he can. If you only will loosen his rein, I am sure he will be able to use all of his power, and he

"Get On, You Lazy Fellow!"

will not be so uncomfortable."

Jakes listened to the woman and loosened my rein. I put my head down and threw my whole weight against the collar. I was finally able to move the load up the hill.

The old woman walked across the footpath and came across the road. She stroked and patted my neck. It was a good feeling to be patted again. She asked Jakes to remember that it was very hard for a horse to pull such a heavy load uphill with a check-rein, and she hoped he wouldn't use it anymore. He nodded in agreement and from then on gave me a loose rein. But even with a loose rein my work loads were too heavy. Every day I grew weaker.

At the end of the day I was placed in a dark stable. Besides being depressing, this lack of light almost ruined my eyesight. I grew more unhappy every day.

The Old Woman Pats Me.

Nicholas Skinner

Chapter 27
Hard Times

As I grew more depressed in my new home, my strength and health began to fail. I was no longer able to do my share of the heavy work, so I was sold again.

My new master owned a fleet of cabs. He was a cruel-looking man with black eyes and a hooked nose. His mouth was hard and unsmiling, and his voice was as harsh as the grinding of cart wheels over graveled stones. His name was Nicholas Skinner.

I have heard people say that seeing is believing; but I would say that feeling is believing. For up until this time I never knew the utter misery of a cab horse's life.

Skinner owned a fleet of shabby cabs, and they were driven by second-rate drivers. He was hard on the men, and they in turn were hard on the horses. In this place, we were given no Sunday rest and had to work long hours in the scorching heat of the summer.

Sometimes on a Sunday morning, I had to drive a group of men out to the country. They would insist upon driving up and down steep hills as fast as possible. After these rides, I was so fevered and worn that I could hardly touch my food. How I longed for the nice bran mash that Jerry used to give me on hot summer nights! I often thought about the cool meals and the Sunday rests that would make my work easier. But in this new job there were no rests and no good food. My new driver was as hard as his master. He had a cruel whip with something so sharp at

Up and Down Steep Hills

the end of it that it sometimes drew blood. He would even whip me under the belly and flip the lash out at my head. All these things made me feel as if life was not worth living. I missed the kind words and soft caresses I had while I lived with Jerry and his family. Here, I was treated as if I was a machine, rather than a living animal with feelings.

My life was now so miserable that I thought many times of Ginger. I too wished I would simply drop dead at my work and be out of my misery. And one day my wish almost came true.

I went on the stand at eight in the morning and had done a good share of work when we had to take a man to the train station. After the man had boarded the train, my driver decided to wait around for some more business. Within a very short time a family of four approached us and asked the driver if we could take them into town. They had a lot of heavy

A Lot of Heavy Luggage

luggage, and while the father began loading the cab, the young girl came around to look at me.

"Papa," she said, "I am sure this poor horse cannot take us and all our bags so far. He looks so weak and worn out, just look at him."

"Oh, he's all right, miss," said my driver. "He is stronger than he looks."

The girl's father looked doubtful, but my driver was so eager to show him that I could do the job that he began to load the heaviest trunks onto the cab. I could hear the springs in the cab strain as he piled on more and more luggage.

The load was very heavy, and I had had neither food nor rest since early that morning. But I did my best, in spite of cruelty and injustice. I was moving along fairly well until we came to a steep hill. My own exhaustion and the heavy load proved to be too much. I

The Girl Sees I Am Weak.

was struggling to keep going, driven on by constant lashes from the whip, when all of a sudden my feet slipped out from under me. I fell to the ground. I lay perfectly still, and I had no power to move. I thought that this was my time to die. There was a confusion around me, and I heard loud, angry voices and the sounds of luggage being unloaded. It was all like a dream. I thought I heard that sweet voice saying:

"Oh, that poor horse! It is all our fault!"

Someone came around and loosened the strap of my bridle and undid the collar. I heard someone say, "He is dead. He'll never get up again." Then I could hear a policeman giving orders, but I did not even open my eyes. I could only draw a gasping breath now and then. Some cold water was thrown over my head, and some liquid was poured into my mouth. I was covered with a blanket, and I lay there on the cold street for a long time.

I Fall to the Ground.

Soon, I felt my life returning. A kind-voiced man was patting me and encouraging me to rise.

After one or two attempts, I staggered to my feet and was gently led to some stables which were nearby. Here, I was put into a comfortable stall and given some warm food.

In the evening I was well enough to be led back to my owner's stables. Early the next morning Mr. Skinner came to look at me.

"This horse has had it," he said. "If we could give him a rest for six months he would be able to work again, but I have no time or money to nurse sick horses. My plan is to work them as long as I can, and then sell them for as much as I can."

So Mr. Skinner decided to give me ten days of rest and good food so that I might look my best for the horse fair.

A Kind Man Encourages Me to Rise.

The Broken-Down Horses

Chapter 28
Farmer Thoroughgood and His Grandson

At this fair I found myself in with all the old broken-down horses. Some were lame, some broken-winded, some old, and some that I am sure it would have been merciful to shoot.

The buyers and sellers did not look much better off than the poor horses. There were poor old men trying to get a horse or a pony for a small amount of money. And there were men trying to sell a worn-out beast for a few dollars. Poverty had hardened these men, and I longed to hear a kind human voice I could trust.

I noticed a man who looked like a farmer. He had a young boy at his side. The farmer had a broad back and round shoulders, his face was kind, and he wore a broad-brimmed hat. When he came up to me I saw a flicker in his eye. I pricked up my ears and looked at him.

"There's a horse, Willie, that has known better days," he said. "Oh yes, my boy, he must have been something when he was young."

He put out his hand and gave me a kind pat on the neck. I put out my nose in answer to his kindness. The boy stroked my face.

"Poor old fellow! See, Grandpa, see how well he understands kindness. Could you buy him and make him young again like you did with Ladybird?"

The boy's grandfather explained that Ladybird had not been an old horse, just a run-down and badly used one. But the boy

Farmer Thoroughgood and Willie

insisted that I too could not be that old, and that I was just worn out and in need of a good rest.

The farmer laughed and felt my legs, which were swollen and strained. He looked at my mouth and soon agreed with his grandson. He offered a few dollars for me, and he and his grandson led me away.

The farmer's name was Mr. Thoroughgood. He gave me to the care of his grandson, Willie. I was given hay and oats every night and morning and the run of the meadow during the day. Willie brought me carrots and spent many hours standing by me and petting me.

I improved steadily. By the spring my legs were well again, and I pulled Willie and his grandfather all the way to town in a fine carriage. Farmer Thoroughgood was very pleased and proud. He and Willie talked it over and decided to find me a good home where I would be loved and valued.

The Farmer Feels My Legs.

Miss Ellen and Her Two Sisters

Chapter 29
My Last Home

One day during the summer the groom cleaned and brushed me with such care that I knew some change was about to happen. Willie was anxious and excited as he got into the carriage with his grandfather.

"If the women like him," said the old man, "they will be happy and so will he."

We traveled for a mile or two until we reached a small house with a lawn and trees in the front. Willie rang the bell, and three elderly women came out of the house. They seemed lively and excited to meet me. One of them, named Miss Ellen, took to me at once. They asked Mr. Thoroughgood many questions about me. He told them that I had been overworked and treated badly, but I was now in fine condition and only needed good treatment and a lot of kindness. The women talked it over and decided to keep me for a while to see how I worked out. Willie gave me a big hug, and his grandfather patted me good-bye.

I was led to my new stable and fed warm food. Soon, a groom came to look me over. He stared at me for a minute and said:

"That star on his face is just like the one Black Beauty had. He is the same height too."

Soon he came to the place in my neck where I had been given an injection a long time ago. He began talking to himself in disbelief.

"White star on the forehead, one white foot, that little patch of white hair on the back. It

Joe Green Recognizes Me.

must be Black Beauty! Beauty! Do you remember me? I'm Joe Green. I was just a boy when I almost killed you by forgetting to cover you on that cold night!"

He began patting me and he was overjoyed. I was very happy, and I put my nose up to him and tried to say that we were friends. I never saw a man so pleased.

After that day, I was taken out almost every afternoon. Miss Ellen and her two sisters soon learned to love me.

I have now lived in this happy place for a whole year. Joe is the best and kindest groom I ever had. My strength and spirit grow every day. Willie and Mr. Thoroughgood come to visit me often, and the women have promised never to sell me. My troubles are all over, and I am finally at home.

My Troubles Are Over.